Alesha
the Acrobat
Fairy

For Cara Holway, with lots of love

Special thanks to
Sue Mongredien

ORCHARD BOOKS
338 Euston Road, London NW1 3BH
Orchard Books Australia
Level 17/207 Kent Street, Sydney, NSW 2000
A Paperback Original

First published in 2011 by Orchard Books

HiT entertainment

A CIP catalogue record for this book is available
from the British Library.

ISBN 978 1 40831 288 9

3 5 7 9 10 8 6 4 2

Printed in Great Britain

The paper and board used in this paperback are natural recyclable
products made from wood grown in sustainable forests. The
manufacturing processes conform to the environmental regulations
of the country of origin.

Orchard Books is a division of Hachette Children's Books,
an Hachette UK company

www.hachette.co.uk

Alesha
the Acrobat
Fairy

by Daisy Meadows

ORCHARD BOOKS

www.rainbowmagic.co.uk

Jack Frost's Ice Castle

Swan Theatre

THE SWAN THEATRE

Funky Feet Dance Studios

Tippington Ice Rink

Who likes talent shows? Not me!
So, goblins, listen carefully,
Each Showtime Fairy has a star,
Their magic glitters near and far.

Now do exactly as I say,
And steal these magical stars away,
Then, when our wicked work is done,
We can spoil all showtime fun!

Contents

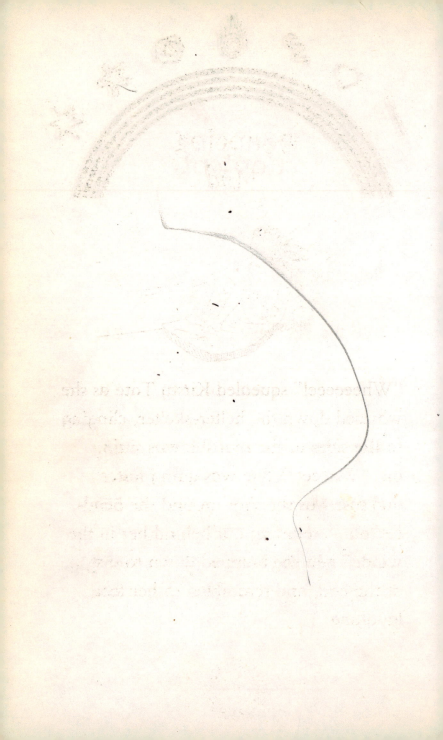

Bouncing Mad

"Wheeeeee!" squealed Kirsty Tate as she whizzed down the helter-skelter, clinging to the sides of the mat she was sitting on. "Wheeee!" She was going faster and faster as she shot around the bends, her hair streaming out behind her in the wind. Then she bumped down to a stop at the end, and scrambled to her feet, laughing.

Kirsty heard another
high-pitched "Wheeeee!"
coming from behind her, and grinned
as her best friend, Rachel Walker, shot
around the last twist of the helter-skelter
and skidded to the end of the slide, too.

"That was so cool!" Rachel said, getting up. "My head's spinning now."

The girls handed their mats to the man in charge and sat on a bench to put their shoes back on. Kirsty was staying with Rachel's family for the half-term holiday,  and today they were back at Tippington Funfair, where they'd had a very exciting time a few days ago. As well as trying out more of the rides today, they'd also come to watch the acrobatic auditions which were being held at the fair. Some students from the local school were taking part, and the girls had offered to help with their special effects.

The winner of today's audition would go through to a big variety show which was to be held at the end of the week.

"I'm glad the rain has stopped," Kirsty said, as they left the helter-skelter. It had been pouring down earlier. "The ground is really wet and muddy though, isn't it? I wish we'd worn wellies."

"Me too," Rachel said, squelching through the boggy ground. She lowered her voice and leaned closer to Kirsty. "If there are any goblins here today, they won't like that at all.

They hate getting their feet wet, don't they?"

Kirsty nodded. "That's true," she said. She glanced around. "I was hoping we might spot a  goblin from the top of the helter-skelter, but I didn't see any, did you?"

"No," Rachel replied. "We'll just have to keep looking. I bet they'll be around here somewhere."

Kirsty and Rachel shared a very exciting secret. They were friends with the fairies, and at the start of the week, they'd been asked to help the Showtime Fairies on a special mission.

The Showtime Fairies had magical
stars on the ends of their wands, which
gave them the power to help fairies
and humans use their particular talents
and skills to their best abilities. But
unfortunately Jack Frost, a mean, spiky
creature, had ordered his goblin servants
to steal the magic stars, and hide them
in the human world. So far, the girls
had helped the fairies recover two of
their stars, but there were still five left to
find. Rachel and Kirsty were very keen
to find the other magic stars, because
without them, people couldn't perform
as well as usual – meaning that the
auditions and variety show might go
horribly wrong!

"I'm sure those goblins will be here
today," Kirsty said as they walked

through the fair. "They won't be able to resist another audition taking place – I bet they'll try and spoil it again."

Rachel nodded. The cheeky goblins had been up to naughty tricks this week by turning up to the auditions and pretending to be from a school called Icy Towers so that they could  take part. They had caused all sorts of trouble, especially for the children who were taking part in the magic show auditions, muddling up their tricks and breaking some of their 'magic' items.

"Maybe we should head straight to the audition tent to see if the goblins are there again," Rachel said.

Kirsty agreed, and the girls began making their way towards the Big Top – a circus tent in which the auditions were taking place. The tent was on the other side of the fair, but they could see the top of its huge stripy dome rising above the rides and stalls that stood in front of it. The girls passed a tombola, and some kiosks selling candyfloss and popcorn.

They were just walking past the queue of people waiting to go on the bouncy castle, when Kirsty noticed a commotion in the crowd, and stopped to watch.

Three children wearing leotards, spangly leggings and sparkly headbands were shoving their way rudely to the front of the queue. "Coming through, coming through, make way," one of them shouted bossily.

"Hey, there's a queue here, you know," a woman said crossly. "You should wait your turn!"

But the children in green completely ignored the woman, and leaped on to the bouncy castle, pushing all the other children off it.

"Yuck," said Rachel, watching them.

"They're making the bouncy castle dirty with their bare feet – they're all muddy!"

"And they're very *big*," Kirsty said suspiciously. "Big feet, big noses, green faces… they're goblins!"

Into the
Big Top

The goblins started bouncing higher and
higher, throwing themselves all over the
bouncy castle. The cross faces of the
people waiting in the queue soon turned
to laughter, as the goblins bounced into
each other, skidded and tumbled over,
then bounced even higher.

Someone started clapping, and the goblins bowed in mid-air. "You should come and cheer for us in the acrobat auditions for the talent show," one of them called out breathlessly. "We're going to do even better stuff there!"

"Yeah!" another added, as he bounced off the side of the castle. "We're going to be AMAZING!"

Rachel and Kirsty were still watching.

"They're having lots of fun, but they don't look quite as acrobatic as I thought they might," Rachel murmured to Kirsty, as one of the goblins knocked another over, and the crowd cheered. "If they've got one of the magic stars, then surely its powers would make them better acrobats than this?"

"Maybe they've lost the star somewhere," Kirsty said thoughtfully. "You know how careless they can be!"

Just then, the goblins bounced right off the bouncy castle, and bowed solemnly to the queue of people who clapped them. The woman running the stall didn't look very happy. "Look at the muddy mess you've left on my bouncy castle!" she fumed as the goblins scampered off, giggling.

"Let's follow them," Kirsty said.

The girls hurried after the goblins, who seemed to be heading in the direction of the Big Top. Kirsty and Rachel kept as close as they could without making it too obvious they were following them.

Luckily, the goblins were so busy
boasting about what wonderful acrobats
they were, an elephant could have
been following and they wouldn't have
noticed!

"It's a shame we lost that magic star,"
one of them said glumly. "We'd be even
better acrobats if we still had it."

"Ahh, we don't need that," a second
goblin assured him. "We're so talented
we can win the audition without a silly
old fairy star."

Kirsty and Rachel
exchanged interested
glances. Aha! So
the goblins *had*
lost the magic star
somewhere – where
on earth could it be?

Just then, they heard shouts behind them. "Rachel! Is that you? Rachel!"

They turned to see a group of children rushing towards them. "Hi guys," Rachel said with a smile. "This is Kirsty." Out of the corner of her eye she could see the goblins disappearing

around the side of a stall. "Kirsty, this is Josie, Maya and Dylan, we go to the same school. They're all taking part in the acrobat auditions later. How have the rehearsals been today?"

"Terrible," Maya said, pulling a face. "Everything went wrong."

"I fell off the high wire," Dylan said glumly.

"And then I didn't quite catch Maya when we were on the trapeze," Josie said with a sigh. "So all three of us ended up falling on to the safety net." She bit her lip. "If we do the same thing at the auditions, we won't stand a chance of getting through to the final."

"I don't know what went wrong," Maya said. "We've been practising for weeks. I thought we had our act spot on... but obviously not."

Kirsty and Rachel looked sympathetic, they both knew exactly why things hadn't gone well for the young acrobats. It was all because Alesha's magic star wasn't where it should be, at the end of her wand. They had to find it again – and fast!

"We're going to the Big Top now," Josie said. "We're meeting Mum there to get ready for the auditions."

"Oh, yes," Rachel said, "we've got to go there too. We're helping out with

the special effects. Let's go together."
She glanced at Kirsty, wishing they had
more time to look for the magic star,
and to keep an eye on the goblins, but
Mrs Evans, the lady who was organising
today's auditions, had asked them to
come along early so that she could show
them what to do.

As they headed for the large tent,
Kirsty and Rachel noticed that the
goblins had gone this way, too, judging
from the large footprints they saw in the
mud every so often. Good – they hadn't
lost them!

Inside the Big Top there was a large,
circular stage surrounded by lots of seats.
It really was big! Above the stage there
were two trapeze swings and a high
wire with a safety net underneath.

There were brightly coloured ribbons and banners all around the arena, and there was an atmosphere of nervous excitement, with last-minute rehearsals taking place.

"There are the judges, look," Josie whispered, pointing to where three grown-ups were having their microphones fitted. "That lady with the black hair is called Maria Moritz. She used to be a trapeze artist herself when she was younger. She's famous!"

Mrs Evans recognised Rachel and hurried over to say hello. "Hi, girls," she said. "Thanks for offering to help with our special effects today. Come with me and I'll show you what to do. Josie, your mum's waiting in the warm-up area. Why don't you, Maya and Dylan start warming up and I'll be with you in a minute."

Rachel and Kirsty followed Mrs Evans up some steps to a platform at the side of the stage, where she showed them a thick, white cord. "This cord is attached to that net above the stage, which is full of silvery glitter," she told them. "When I give you the signal, your job is to pull the cord, and send glitter showering down over the acrobats. OK?"

"No problem," Rachel said politely. She and Kirsty grinned at each other. It would be exciting, the two of them being up on the platform for the auditions – and they would get a great view of everything… including any goblin mischief!

Mrs Evans went to sort out her acrobats, leaving Kirsty and Rachel alone. Then Kirsty blinked in surprise. "Rachel," she hissed, pointing at the net of glitter suspended above them. "Look – something's moving up there."

There was a flurry of silver sparkles inside the net as both girls watched… and then, out flew a tiny fairy. Rachel smiled. "It's Alesha the Acrobat Fairy!" she cried happily.

Follow those Footprints!

Alesha soared down towards the girls and hovered in mid-air before them. "Hello again!" she said. Kirsty and Rachel had met all seven of the Showtime Fairies on the first day of their holiday. Alesha was very pretty, with dark hair covered in sparkles, and her bright pink leotard covered in patterns.

"Hi," Kirsty smiled. "We've already spotted the goblins who had your star," she told Alesha. "Unfortunately, they seem to have lost it somewhere."

"It's definitely nearby," Alesha said. "I can sense it. I was just looking in that net of glitter for it, but it wasn't there."

"Where might the goblins have lost it?" Rachel wondered aloud.

Kirsty was thinking hard. "Whenever I've lost something, my mum always tells me to retrace my steps," she said. "To go back to all the places I've been since I last had it. So maybe if we retraced the *goblins'* footsteps..." She broke off.

"Ahh. We don't know where they've been all day."

"But we can track their footprints in the mud and find out!" Rachel realised. "The goblins have such big feet, they're sure to leave lots of prints behind."

"Good thinking," Alesha said. "I'll turn you both into fairies and we can fly around the fair together, following the footprints. With a bit of luck, we'll see my magic star on the way."

Alesha hid herself in Rachel's pocket as Kirsty and Rachel climbed down from the platform.

Then the girls ducked behind one of the
big stage curtains so that they were out
of sight. They couldn't let anyone see
Alesha working her fairy magic!

Alesha waved her wand, and a swirl
of magical sparkles streamed from its tip
all around the two girls.

They felt themselves
shrinking
smaller until
they were
the same
size as
their fairy
friend –
and they
had their own
fairy wings on
their backs, too!

The three fairies fluttered their glimmering wings and flew up to the highest point of the Big Top where nobody would see them. Alesha showed them a gap in the roof of the tent, and out they flew into the open air, way above the crowds.

"Let's head for the bouncy castle," Rachel said, pointing it out below them. "We know they'd already lost the magic star by the time they got there, so we need to trace their steps from before they started bouncing."

They flew down towards the bouncy castle in a line, and Kirsty realised that she was smiling to herself. She so loved being able to fly. It was even better than whizzing down the helter-skelter! They landed on one of the turrets of the bouncy castle and peered down to the ground. "There are the goblins' footprints," Kirsty said, spotting them in the mud. "It looks as though they came from the direction of the coconut shy. Let's search around there."

40

Down they flew towards the coconut shy, making sure they didn't fly too low. There were so many people at the fair, they had to be careful they weren't  spotted by anybody. The existence of Fairyland was a secret, and Rachel and Kirsty were the only two humans ever to have been there, or to know about it. They knew how important it was for it to stay this way, too!

They searched around the coconut shy,
but there was no sign of any star.
"I don't think it's here," Alesha said.
"I'm sure I would sense it, if it was.
Where do the tracks lead next?"

Rachel was rather relieved to be
leaving the coconut shy behind. It was
a dangerous place for a fairy, with so
many colourful balls being thrown at
the coconuts!

"This way," she
said, pointing out
some more tracks.
These tracks
led to the lucky
dip, which was a huge
barrel of colourful strips of paper, with
lots of wrapped-up presents hidden
inside.

When nobody was looking, the three fairies dived into the barrel and began searching through the paper strips, but there was no star there either.

"Oh, where is it?" Alesha sighed anxiously. "If we don't find it soon, the acrobat auditions are going to be a disaster. We've got to get our hands on that magic star!"

Star Turn

Clambering out, the three fairies
followed the goblin tracks further back.
"Wouldn't you know it?" Kirsty groaned
as she realised which way they were
heading. "We're going back to where
we started – the Big Top!"

"I suppose it makes sense," Rachel said, fluttering inside the roof of the Big Top and finding herself above the backstage area. "The goblins would have come here to rehearse earlier, so they might easily have lost the star then."

"Well, let's—" Alesha began, but then she broke off and her body stiffened suddenly, as they all heard the sound of voices. Not just any voices either – but harsh, boastful voices. Goblins!

"The talent has arrived, make way for the talent," one of the goblins shouted, hurrying into the backstage area and snatching some acrobat ribbons. "Come on, let's get our stuff ready. It's nearly time to hit the stage."

"Cool!" another goblin crowed, picking up a set of juggling balls. A third goblin grabbed a pile of hula hoops.

Then everyone – goblins, people and fairies – jumped as the tannoy crackled, and a voice came over the speakers.

"The auditions will start in three minutes. Could everyone please take their seats? Thank you."

"Three minutes! Brilliant," the goblin with the hula hoops cheered. "I can't wait to get out there and do our stuff. We are *so* going to win this, boys!"

"You know it," the goblin with the juggling balls said, high-fiving him and dropping all the balls on the floor. The others helped him pick them up again and they all rushed towards the main stage, still bragging about how fantastic they were going to be.

Meanwhile, the three fairies were feeling anxious. Just minutes to go before the show started, and they still hadn't found Alesha's magic star!

"Kirsty and I have got to get ready to do our special effects for the show now," Rachel said helplessly. She sighed. "I can't believe we've run out of time!"

Alesha turned them back into girls and slipped into Rachel's pocket. "Well, the show hasn't started just yet," she said optimistically. "You never know, we still might find my star somewhere."

Kirsty and Rachel hurried to their position on the platform, their hearts pounding. The auditions were going to be so awful if the star wasn't found in time! But where could it be?

The audience had taken their seats now, and applauded as the judges walked to their seats. "Good afternoon, everyone!" said Maria Moritz, the judge who Josie had recognised. She had a large upturned top hat in front of her.

"We have put the names of all the contestants in here, and I will now pick our first acrobats to perform. They are the students from…" She reached in and pulled out a name. "Icy Towers!"

"The goblins!" Rachel and Kirsty both whispered, feeling sick with nerves as the three goblins ran on stage, all looking very excited.

The audience clapped, and then a hush fell as the audition began. The goblins started their act very dramatically with a routine of tumbling flips, cartwheels and handsprings, which finished with one goblin flipping right on to the other two goblins' shoulders. Everyone applauded wildly as he balanced there perfectly, before all three of them went springing into more back flips towards the sides of the stage. Once there, they climbed up to the trapeze swings and the high wire.

"Wow," Alesha said, peeping out of Rachel's pocket. "So far they're really good."

"I don't remember Josie, Maya and Dylan being as good as this when I saw them at school," Rachel said, feeling worried. *What if the goblins won?* she was thinking uneasily. Surely somebody would notice that they were goblins, and the whole secret of Fairyland would come out? They couldn't let that happen!

"Look at them now," Kirsty breathed, her eyes glued to the stage.

Star Turn

Two of the goblins were swinging on
the flying trapeze, while the
other walked carefully
along the high wire.
She bit her lip.
"They're *so*
much better
than when
they were on
the bouncy
castle, aren't
they? Which
must mean…"
Both girls said
the next words
together as they
realised at the exact same
moment what had happened.
"They've found the star!"

Glitter
Shower

Rachel, Kirsty and Alesha stared harder
than ever at the acrobat goblins, hoping
to spot the magic star somewhere. Had
one of them tucked it in their leotard,
maybe? It certainly wasn't in their hands,
and they didn't have any pockets in
which they could have hidden it.

In the next moment, the goblin on the high wire somersaulted neatly down to the ground, and took two of the long acrobat ribbons they'd brought on stage. He pranced along, waving and twirling the ribbons energetically, making them curl and spin into different shapes. The audience all seemed transfixed, their eyes glued to the twirling ribbons.

Kirsty, Rachel and Alesha were watching the ribbon display too – and all of a sudden, Alesha gave a gasp and pointed her finger excitedly. "Look! At the end of the red ribbon – it's my star!"

Kirsty and Rachel immediately turned to look at the red ribbon – and saw that yes, sure enough, there was a small rainbow-coloured star attached to its end. The star was shimmering and twinkling with magical sparkles.

Then the goblin gave the ribbons a flick… and the girls and Alesha saw the star fly off the end of the red ribbon and go sailing through the air.

"It's come off!" Kirsty gasped.

The goblins had noticed this, too. One of them cried out in alarm as the star fell on to the safety net and bounced up into the air.

The goblin who'd been twirling the ribbons dropped them abruptly and scrambled on to the safety net. The audience seemed confused. "Is he meant to be doing that?" Rachel heard somebody muttering. "Is this part of the act?"

The goblin seemed to have forgotten all about the audition though – he just wanted that magic star back. He bounced across the net towards it – but as he bounced up, the star bounced down, out of his reach. Then, when he bounced down again, the star bounced up! Both of the other goblins dropped from their swings to try and help, making the star bounce even higher as they landed on the net.

The judges didn't seem impressed.
"Do they think the safety net is a
trampoline?" Maria Moritz murmured
disapprovingly.

"They're going to catch that star any
second," Rachel hissed, as the goblins all
bounced up and down, lunging at the
star and falling over as they
missed it. "What can we do?"

"I've got an idea,"
Kirsty said, and
promptly pulled on
the cord to release the
glitter from its net above
the goblins. Down fell the
silver glitter like shiny,
sparkly snowflakes,
landing all over the
goblins and the safety net.

"Alesha, can you turn us back into
fairies?" she asked quickly. "The glitter
will camouflage us, and we can
fly down to get the star!"

Alesha thought this was a wonderful
idea! She quickly waved her wand, and
her fairy magic made Kirsty and Rachel
shrink down to fairy-size once more.

Then all three
of them
zoomed
through
the cloud
of falling
glitter
towards the
safety net,
hoping to spot
the magic star.

But the goblins were hoping the same thing of course, and they were scrabbling around in the mist of sparkles, still hunting desperately for it.

"Where's that stupid star?" one of them wailed. "I can't see it anywhere now there's all this glittery stuff flying about!"

Kirsty's heart pounded at the words. This was their chance to find the star before the goblins did. They had to get it!

Then she heard Rachel's excited voice. "There's the star!"

Catch a Falling Star!

Rachel had spotted the star bouncing up from the safety net and flew quickly to catch it, but somehow she missed it, and it fell back down to the net.

Then, when the star bounced up again, Alesha made a grab for it... but only got a handful of glitter.

Down bounced the magic star again,
and up it flew. This time Kirsty zoomed
over and seized it, and gave a little yelp
of triumph.
"Got it!"
she cried.
Rachel
and
Alesha
both
flew over
to help her
with it, because
it was big and heavy

for one tiny fairy to carry. All three of
them flew the star to the platform once
more, where Alesha magically turned it
back to Fairyland size and fitted it in its
rightful place, on the end of her wand.

Its rainbow colours shone brightly, and the girls could see it had a picture of a trapeze swing on it.

"Hurrah!" Alesha cheered, her pretty little face alight with satisfaction. She waved her wand in a pattern in the air, and some rainbow-coloured sparkles shimmered from its tip. Then she smiled happily at Kirsty and Rachel. "There," she said. "Now the auditions will be a success. Thank you, girls!"

The three fairies hugged each other joyfully. They'd done it!

Then Alesha waved her wand again, turning Rachel and Kirsty back into girls.

Down below, the goblins were still bouncing about on the safety net. They were having such a good time, pushing each other over and giggling as they bounced up and down that they seemed to have forgotten all about finding the magic star. "This is even more fun than the bouncy castle!" one goblin whooped, making the audience laugh.

Even the judges were smiling, too! Then, when the goblins were too exhausted to bounce any more, and just lay giggling on the safety net, everyone clapped them.

"Well, that was certainly different," Maria Moritz said afterwards, raising an eyebrow.

"The next school to perform," said Maria, smiling and reaching into the hat, "is....
Tippington!"

Rachel gasped in excitement. "Fingers crossed, guys!" she said.

Alesha smiled. "They'll be fine," she assured Rachel. "My star will make sure their talent shines through! I'll fill up the net with glitter again though," she said, as Josie, Maya and Dylan all ran on stage.

Alesha waved her wand, and the girls saw some magical sparkles flicker around the glitter net... and then, in the blink of an eye, it was full once more.

"I'd better go," Alesha said, kissing Kirsty and Rachel goodbye – tiny, tickly fairy kisses on their faces.

"Goodbye – and thanks again!"

"It was fun," Kirsty said. "Goodbye, Alesha!"

Then Kirsty and Rachel watched as Josie, Maya and Dylan began their act. The girls swung out on their trapezes, while Dylan stepped confidently on to the high wire.

Down below, Mrs Evans gave the girls the thumbs-up sign and they pulled the cord together.

Down tumbled the glitter… only this time it shimmered and sparkled all the colours of the rainbow, as it fell over the acrobats. "Ooooh!" the audience marvelled. "Isn't that beautiful?"

Rachel and Kirsty looked at each other and smiled. It was the perfect magical ending to a perfectly magical day!

Now it's time for Kirsty and Rachel to help...

Darcey the Dance Diva Fairy

Read on for a sneak peek...

"The Funky Feet Dance Studios," Kirsty read out as she stared up at the pink and blue neon sign on top of the modern glass and steel building. She grinned. "That's a *brilliant* name for a dance studio, isn't it, Rachel?"

Rachel laughed. "Yes, it makes you feel like dancing, doesn't it? Look, Kirsty, the Tippington School team is already here." And she pointed at the school minibus in the car park. "We should be just in time to see them rehearse before they take part in the dance auditions."

Every day during the half-term holiday

local schools, including Rachel's, were taking part in auditions in magic, drama, acrobatics, dance, singing and ice skating.

The Tippington Variety Show was being held at the end of half-term week, and the organisers were choosing the best acts to perform in the show. The money raised would be used to pay for an adventure playground, a bandstand and an outdoor theatre in the town's Oval Park...

Read Darcey the Dance Diva Fairy
to find out what adventures are in store for
Kirsty and Rachel!

Meet the
Showtime Fairies

Collect them all to find out how Kirsty and
Rachel help their magical friends to save
the Tippington Variety Show!

www.rainbowmagicbooks.co.uk

Meet the fairies, play games
and get sneak peeks at
the latest books!

www.rainbowmagicbooks.co.uk

There's fairy fun for everyone at
www.rainbowmagicbooks.co.uk.
You'll find great activities, competitions, stories and
fairy profiles, and also a special newsletter.

Competition!

If you study these four pictures of Darcey the Dance Diva Fairy very carefully you'll see that one of them is slightly different from the others. Can you work out which one is the odd one out? Make a note of the name of this book and the letter and when you have enjoyed all seven books in the Showtime Fairies series, send the answers in to us!

A

B

C

D

We will put all of the correct entries into a draw and select one winner to receive a special **Rainbow Magic Showtime Fairies Pack** featuring lots of treats!

Enter online now at

www.rainbowmagicbooks.co.uk

No purchase required. Only one entry per child. Two prize draws will take place on 29 July 2011 and 28 October 2011. Alternatively, readers can send the seven answers on a postcard to: Rainbow Magic Showtime Fairies Competition, Orchard Books, 338 Euston Road, London NW1 3BH. Australian readers can write to: Rainbow Magic Showtime Fairies Competition, Hachette Children's Books, level 17/207 Kent St, Sydney, NSW 2000. E-mail: childrens.books@hachette.com.au

Meet the Princess Fairies

Jack Frost has stolen the Princess Fairies'
tiaras. Kirsty and Rachel must get them back
before all the magic in the world fades away!

www.rainbowmagicbooks.co.uk